THIS BOOK BELONGS TO

_____

I celebrated **World Book Day 2020**
with this gift from my local bookseller and
Orion Children's Books.

#ShareAStory

The Day We Met the Queen

ONJALI Q. RAÚF

Orion

ORION CHILDREN'S BOOKS

First published in Great Britain in 2020
by Hodder and Stoughton

1 3 5 7 9 10 8 6 4 2

A CIP catalogue record for this book
is available from the British Library.

ISBN 978 1 51010 815 8
ISNB (Export) 978 1 51010 816 5

Printed and bound in Great Britain by Clays Ltd, Elcograf S.p.A.

The paper and board used in this book are made
from wood from responsible sources.

Orion Children's Books
An imprint of
Hachette Children's Group
Part of Hodder and Stoughton
Carmelite House
50 Victoria Embankment
London EC4Y 0DZ

An Hachette UK Company

www.hachette.co.uk
www.hachettechildrens.co.uk

A VERY ROYAL ASSEMBLY

'Can you believe it? Can you *believe* we're going to see the Queen tomorrow in *actual* real life!'

I looked at Michael. We were standing by the bus stop, waiting for Tom and Josie. Michael pushed his glasses even farther up his nose and, holding the card to the light, stared at it hard – just like shopkeepers do when they think your money isn't real.

But we both knew the invitation *was* real.

The card was so thick it wouldn't let any light through. The writing was fancy and swirly and there was a thick blob of shiny red wax on the envelope. All those things reminded us that the actual real-life Queen of England had sent it and was expecting us to join her for tea tomorrow.

I got my own invitation out from my rucksack and held it up to the light too. Not because I wanted to check if it was real, but because I wanted to look as important as Michael did. Holding stuff up to the light always makes things seem more serious and scientific than just looking down at them in your hands. I guess that's why people in detective programmes on the telly are always doing it, even when the room they're in is dark and holding something up doesn't make a single bit of difference.

'Hey!' called Tom as he hurried towards us. Josie was following him and waving as she dribbled her football. Tom's blond hair was so spiky today it made his head look as if lots of tiny, shiny pyramids had suddenly sprouted up on top of it. Josie's red hair was in a short, thick plait, which looked like a piece of twisted boat rope that someone had cut off in the middle. You knew it was an important day if Josie's hair was in a plait, because she hates her hair being touched or brushed almost as much as she hates beetroot.

'You look . . . different,' said Michael, staring

2

at Josie's hair as if he wasn't quite sure what she had done to herself.

Josie shrugged. 'It's for the assembly. Mum and Dad promised me tickets to the West Ham game next week if I let them plait it, so I thought I might as well. Even if it does make me look stupid. I mean, look at it!' Grabbing the end of the plait, she pulled it around the back of her neck and over her shoulder to try and make it reach her mouth. But it was too short. 'What's the point of it?' she asked, shaking her head. For Josie, hair only existed for one reason – so that you could suck on the ends of it when you were nervous or needed help thinking. And to do that, hair needed to be loose and free – and unbrushed.

'Did you bring your invitations?' I asked.

Tom nodded and reached up to check his hair was still super spiky. 'Mine's in my bag. But . . .' Dropping his arms, he scowled and added in a whisper, 'Mum framed it!'

Josie sniggered. 'What? What for?'

'I don't know.' Tom shrugged. 'She said anything from anyone royal should always be

3

framed. Especially something from the Queen. She even framed the envelope!'

'Oh . . .' said Michael, looking down at his frameless invitation as if it was suddenly a disappointment.

'Do you have the list of questions?' asked Tom, looking at me.

I nodded and patted my backpack. Ever since we had known we were going to have tea with the Queen of England, me and Tom and Ahmet and Michael and Josie had spent nearly every break-time writing down all the questions we wanted to ask her. In the end, we had fifty-two questions ready, but then our teacher, Mrs Khan, had said maybe we should cut it down to just two questions each – because the Queen was nearly one hundred years old, and being asked fifty-two questions might make her fall into a coma. Now we were going to read out the questions in morning assembly and show everyone our invitations and explain why we were going to see the Queen. It made my stomach feel funny every time I thought about it.

'Bus is coming!' said Josie, picking up her football and joining the long queue of people in front of us. I put my invitation away carefully between two of my exercise books and, quickly zipping up my rucksack, jumped on board the bus to school. Running up the stairs, we made our way to the front seats.

'Hope Ahmet remembers to bring his invitation,' I said, as I squished up next to Tom. 'Do you think his foster mum will frame his too? His is probably even more special than ours.'

Tom shrugged. 'Maybe . . .'

'Anyone else really nervous?' asked Josie, pulling her plait again and trying even harder to make it reach her mouth. 'I keep worrying I'll forget everything. I hate assemblies . . .'

Me and Michael and Tom fell quiet, because we were all starting to feel nervous too. None of us had ever been asked to get up in front of the whole entire school and speak at an assembly before.

Usually assembly was the best part of the day – because you could just sit and pretend to listen even if sometimes you weren't listening at all. Even the teachers like assembly because they don't have to be working or trying to keep everyone under control. You can tell that teachers love assembly more than anything else because they always want to get there early and then when it starts, they sit and smile as if they're thinking about something much more fun than what they're actually listening to.

But today, instead of Mrs Sanders, our head teacher, staring out at us through her big, square glasses, me and Tom and Josie and Michael and Ahmet were going to be the ones on stage in the huge main hall. All because the Most Famous Woman on the Whole Entire Planet had invited us to her palace for tea.

And that was because of Ahmet, the Most Famous Refugee Boy in the World, who had not only let us be his friends, but had made every single one of us almost as famous as he was. Just because we had tried to help him find his family and stop the Queen and the government from closing the gates and borders to refugees like him.

I hadn't thought any of those things would make us famous. But for some reason, grown-ups get excited about things that should be normal, and that makes you famous somehow.

'As long as I don't forget what I'm supposed to say and go blank, I don't care what happens,' said Tom. 'There is *nothing* worse than going blank! One time, back in New York, I was supposed to sing the national anthem on my own – and I went blank for so long I got booed at! It's probably a good thing we moved to England straight after.'

'Yeah,' said Michael. 'Going blank is bad! But so is sweating . . .' Touching his forehead, he wiped away a big bead of sweat that had appeared.

'I don't want to go red,' said Josie, touching her pale, freckly cheeks. 'If my face goes red on television, I'll have to move to another country – like you did, Tom!'

I wished Josie hadn't reminded me that we were going to be on television too. Standing up on stage and talking in front of the whole school was scary enough, but knowing that lots of people would be filming us too made it feel ten times worse. Now that Ahmet was the Most Famous Refugee Boy in the World, millions of people had found out that we were going to Buckingham Palace for tea with the Queen, and a lot of reporters from the World's Press wanted to film our assembly for the news. So Mrs Sanders was letting them – which meant we were probably going to be on every news channel in the country.

Mrs Khan, who is the best teacher anyone could ever have, said we should try and pretend the reporters weren't there, and that would make doing the assembly easy. But I don't know how anyone can pretend something isn't there when it is. Especially when the something is real people with cameras who are going to be staring at you! It's always easier for me to imagine things *are* there when they aren't – not the other way around. My imagination isn't strong enough to make real things disappear.

Looking at Michael and Josie, I started to wonder which was worse – going red or going blank or sweating so much it looked like you'd been caught in the rain. I couldn't decide, so I told my brain to try not to do any of them.

'Did you all practise again at home yesterday?' I asked. 'I did and Mum said I was good, but that I should stand up straighter.'

Everyone nodded, except Tom.

'I tried,' he explained. 'I mean, I wanted to . . . but you know . . . brothers . . .'

Josie gave him a pat on the shoulder. Tom has more older brothers than should be allowed, and they never leave him alone. He has to share a room with two of them, and the main things they like doing are play-fighting and teasing him and stealing his food, which they do all of the time. I've heard grown-ups tell Tom he's lucky to be the youngest brother. But I don't think Tom feels that way at all.

As the bus came to a stop and we got off and made our way towards the school gates, I told myself that everything was going to be fine. After all, Mrs Sanders had told us exactly what she wanted us to talk about: why the Queen had invited us and what we were going to say to her. And Mrs Khan had helped us write everything out and had let us stay in at break-times all week to practise too. I had copied out our Ten Important Questions in my best handwriting so that we could read them clearly. And Ms Hemsi, Ahmet's special teacher who could speak Kurdish just like he did, had helped him practise his part of the presentation in English, so that he could say why it was so special that the Real Queen of England wanted to meet him.

There were only two things that could spoil any of it. The first was if one of us forgot to speak when it was our turn. But the second thing was even worse: and that was if Brendan-the-Bully decided to do something bad to Ahmet in front of the whole school and the World's Press. I hoped he wouldn't, but you can never be too sure with bullies. Especially not one who hated Ahmet so much that he nearly got expelled because of it.

THE REVENGE THAT STUNK

Brendan-the-Bully hates Ahmet. And me. And Michael. And Tom. And Josie. In fact, I think he might hate everyone, but he hates us the most, because a few weeks ago he got caught calling Ahmet so many horrible names that he nearly got expelled. It wasn't our fault that happened, but bullies don't care if things are your fault or not – they just need someone to blame. So Brendan-the-Bully blamed all of us, but he blamed Ahmet the most. That was why I knew I had to keep a close eye on him and make sure he didn't do anything to ruin the assembly or our trip to see the Queen.

When we got into school, we made our way to the classroom. Ahmet wasn't there but as we were sitting down at our tables, he ran in and sat next to Ms Hemsi, his special teacher, at the back of the class. I gave him a quick wave and he gave me one back.

After that, everything began to feel strange and normal all at the same time. Mrs Khan started to call the register, just like she always did, but instead of saying 'Here, Miss,' in bored voices, everyone answered their names in a jumpier way than usual – as if they had ants in their pants that were making them shuffle in their seats and look back at the five of us. I noticed Brendan-the-Bully and his two best friends Chris and Liam looking back too. But instead of scrunching up their faces at us like they usually did, they were laughing and whispering.

Ahmet didn't seem to notice that everyone was looking at all of us, but Josie's face was now so red and blotchy that it looked like a pizza, and Michael was sweating so much that even his glasses were steaming up. He also looked as if he was having a competition with Tom to see who could touch his hair the most. Tom kept patting his bright blond spikes every few seconds as if to check they were still there, and Michael kept poking at his bubbly Afro as if wanting to make sure it wasn't melting. I could feel my ears burning and my heart thumping inside them as I waited for Mrs Khan to finish the register.

After what seemed like three years, she finally did, and told me and Ahmet and Tom and Josie and Michael that we could leave early, and that Ms Hemsi could go with us too. We grabbed our notes and our royal invitations and Ahmet grabbed his bright red rucksack. It still smelled of old baked beans – even though his foster mum had washed the bag with extra-strong washing-up liquid at least nine times. That meant every time Ahmet picked up his bag, he had to smell that horrible smell and was forced to remember the time when Brendan-the-Bully had poured huge cans of baked beans inside it, just to be mean to someone who was a refugee. I guess there are some bad smells and memories that not even washing-up liquid can get rid of.

'How are you all feeling?' asked Ms Hemsi, as we hurried down the corridor towards the main hall.

'OK,' said Tom, his voice sounding extra squeaky.

We all nodded in agreement, but I knew we weren't really OK at all. Only Ahmet looked as if he was actually happy and not pretend-happy. He was holding his invitation out in front of him carefully, as if it was made of glass, and smiling. I wondered if back in his school in Syria, he was used to doing lots of assemblies. Maybe before the war had started and he'd had to run away, he had stood on a stage and spoken to his whole school lots of times. I told my brain to remember to ask him later, or to ask Ms Hemsi to ask him for me.

'Ah, there you are, kids! Good morning, good morning,' cried out Mrs Sanders, as we walked through the large double doors leading into the main hall. There were long lines of people with cameras standing in front of all the walls. Mrs Sanders came over to us and made us walk quickly past the reporters and cameras that were now clicking and flashing and whispering at us. They made Michael so nervous that he tripped up the stairs and Josie nearly dropped her invitation, but they each pretended as if they hadn't done either of those things. We hurried to the side of the stage and stood behind the large, red velvet curtains that were hanging there. It felt good to get away from all the shining eyes and lenses, even though I knew they were waiting for us.

'Woah,' whispered Tom, as he peeked out from behind the curtains. 'I've never seen so many cameras! Not even when we first got famous!'

'They are here because the Queen, she is our friend now! Yes?' asked Ahmet, nudging me with his elbow and grinning.

I smiled back at him and then peeked out through the curtain too. I wanted to see if there were any reporters that looked like Tintin because if there were, then maybe they would be nicer to us than the reporters who had made up stories about us when we became famous the first time around. But there wasn't a single reporter that looked like Tintin. Not even by a little bit. Most of them were wearing smart suits and shiny shoes and looked like people who worked in banks and offices.

I'm pretty sure those kinds of reporters aren't very much fun. If I do ever become a reporter when

I grow up, I want to be like Tintin and wear a raincoat and scruffy clothes and go on adventures with a pet dog named Snowy. Only in my case, the pet will need to be a hamster or a parrot or a boa constrictor – or something else that I'm not allergic to, but which can still be clever and save my life when I need it to. And even though I can't have a dog, I still want to be as brave and as friendly to everyone as Tintin is. And I definitely *don't* want to be like one of the horrible reporters that pick on people.

Ever since Ahmet made us famous, I've learned that not all reporters care about being friendly or even about telling the truth. I know because they've called Ahmet things that I don't really understand but which I can tell right away aren't nice. Words like 'fraudulent' and 'illegal immigrant' – which are grown-up ways of saying they don't like him. Some of them even said mean lies about me and Tom too! But Mum says that we should feel sorry for bad reporters because lying makes their words empty, and one day no one will believe anything they say. I had never thought of words as things that could be full or empty before, but Mum's a librarian who's read at least fifty-nine thousand books, so she knows all about everything.

After a few minutes, I snuck another look and saw the hall doors opening and classes walking in to fill up the rows of chairs that were waiting for them like train seats.

Mrs Sanders came running up the steps of the stage. 'No need to be nervous,' she said, peering at us over the top of her glasses. 'You'll all be brilliant. Just remember to speak as loudly and as clearly as you can, and most important of all, to have fun!'

I could hear Michael gulping loudly, as if fun wasn't something he was ever going to have again, and Tom tapping his framed invitation against his knees. I wonder why teachers and parents always tell you to have fun when you're about to do the scariest and most least fun thing you could ever do!

'Let's practise one more time!' whispered Josie, her face now so red and so blotchy that she looked like a can of minestrone soup.

I nodded and, blinking my eyes so that they would focus, got out our list of questions. I looked down at them and hoped they would help me remember everything I had to say.

The list looked like this:

The 10 Most Important Questions to Ask the Queen of England (which we cut down from 52 Almost As Important Questions)

1. Have you ever met anyone who's more famous than you? (Tom)
2. What's your favourite football team? (Josie)
3. How heavy is your crown and does it give you a Head Ache when you're wearing it? (Michael)
4. What's your favourite fruit? (Ahmet)
5. If you weren't the Queen, what would you have wanted to be? Would you have liked to be an astronaut maybe (because of all the star medals you wear)? (Me)
6. Who's the Lord Chamberlain that wrote our invitations, and can you do his job even if you

have bad handwriting? (Tom)

7. How does it feel using money and stamps and things with your face on it, and do you like your picture or do you wish you could change it? (Josie)

8. Have you ever been to Disneyland? And did you get to go on all the rides for free because you're the Queen? (Michael)

9. How many handbags do you have and which one would you take with you if you had to run away from a war? (Ahmet)

10. Will you help more children like Ahmet stay safe and find their families until all the wars end? (Me and everyone)

'OK, you lot! Ready?' asked Mrs Sanders. And before any of us could shake our heads with a yes or a no, she stepped out on to the stage and, clapping her hands, shouted, 'QUIET, EVERYONE!'

Instantly, the hall fell silent.

'Good morning, school!'

Everyone shouted back, 'Good morning, Mrs Saaaaan-ders!'

Mrs Sanders nodded proudly and, clasping her

hands together, looked out at everyone.

'Tomorrow, as you all know, five of your fellow students will be off to Buckingham Palace to meet the Queen and join her for what I imagine will be a rather wonderful tea!'

Someone cried out 'Wooooohoooooooo!' which made everyone else giggle and laugh.

'Yes! Woooohooooo indeed,' said Mrs Sanders, smiling. 'Now, Ahmet and his friends have been invited to meet the Queen because they did something extraordinarily brave and kind to help each other. And since we are a School of Sanctuary which values acts of kindness and courage, I am sure you are all as proud of your fellow schoolmates as I am. So instead of me boring you with all the details, I'm going to ask them to come out to tell you all about it – and show you the messages they have received from the Queen!'

Everyone began to clap and cheer and whoop, and Mrs Sanders waved us out on to the stage. My ears felt like they were full of cotton wool and my head was fizzing like a big ball of electricity as I followed Ahmet out and stood next to him.

I looked out, but instead of seeing faces I knew, I saw an ocean of eyeballs blinking back at me.

'Ahmet, you're first. Off you go!' said Mrs Sanders. She gave him a little pat and walked off to the side of the stage.

I watched as Ahmet looked over his shoulder at Ms Hemsi, who was giving him a double thumbs up. He took a step forward. Flicking his hair out of the way, he looked out at the school with his grey-brown lion eyes and opened his mouth.

'Tomorrow, I will go and I will see the Queen of England,' he shouted. 'Because she invite me to her house!'

He took another step forwards and held up the invitation, showing everyone the message the Queen had sent him. His invitation was different from the rest of ours because after his name, the Queen had written out 'The Bravest Refugee Boy I Know' after it.

'In Syria, when we go to friend's house, we bring . . .' Ahmet stopped and tried to remember the word he needed. Everyone waited and I could feel my mouth wanting to yell the word out for him.

'GIFTS!' shouted Ahmet, suddenly remembering. 'We bring gifts of . . . sweets . . . and chocolates . . . so we can share with tea! So, when I meet Queen, I will give her sweets with lemon so she can share. And I will show her this.'

Ahmet lifted up his rucksack and held it up. I could see some people were frowning and whispering and looking confused, but they fell quiet when Ahmet opened his mouth again.

'This bag come with me from Syria . . . and it was GIFT from my dad. So I think Queen will like to see it and I will let her hold it so she can see everything inside it, and I will tell her to not smell it—'

'EEEEEEEEEEEEEEEEEEEEEEEEEEEEEE WWWWWWWWWWWWWWWW!' screeched a girl from the back of the hall.

'UUUUUUUUUUUUGHHHHHHHHH!' cried a boy a second later.

'WHAT'S THAT SMELL?' yelled someone else from the middle of the hall.

The whole hall turned to look in different directions as people began to jump up from their seats with their hands over their mouths, squealing.

'STIIIIIIIIINK BOOOOOOOOOOOOOOMB!' came the answer from someone near the back, and instantly everyone who hadn't already stood up, jumped from their seats.

In less than a second, the whole hall had changed from a sea of eyes to a blurry rush of bodies running in different directions, as teachers and children tried to get away from the disgusting smell.

But there wasn't just one disgusting smell! There were lots! Every few seconds, a new wave of terrible smells seemed to be coming from a different part of the hall. Mrs Sanders had run back on to the stage and was trying to hold her nose and tell people to calm down at the same time.

'I'm going to die!' came a cry.

'We – got – a – get – ouwwa heeeeeere!' shouted a boy with his school jumper over his head.

'Miss! Miss! Look!' screamed a girl, pointing at the boy next to her who had began to heave and howl as if there was a river about to burst out of him. 'He's going to be sick!'

I knew me and Josie and Tom and Michael and Ahmet should have moved and run too, but we couldn't. It was as if our feet were superglued to the floor, and our eyes couldn't stop staring. It was strange watching everything from high up on the stage – even though we could smell the horrible smells, it felt as if we weren't a part of the school any more and all we could do was stand and watch as everyone screamed and ran in different directions and crashed into each other like bumper cars.

'ORDEEEEEEEEEEEEEEEEEEEEEEEEER!' shouted Mrs Sanders, clapping her hands together and trying not to cough. From around the hall, we could see teachers pushing past the shocked reporters and frantically opening doors and windows.

'TEACHERS! TAKE YOUR CLASSES BACK IN AN ORDERLY FASHION TO YOUR CLASSROOMS! QUICKLY, PLEASE!'

Another stink bomb puffed into the air, making

everyone squeal again – although now, some of the squeals sounded more excited and happy than shocked and disgusted. As the classes left line by line, Mrs Sanders hurried over to us.

'I'm sorry, kids, you'll have to get back to class – assembly is over, I'm afraid!'

'Oh!' said Tom, sounding disappointed. 'That sucks!'

'We are not telling about this any more?' asked Ahmet, looking at me. His lion eyes were getting bigger and bigger, and I knew he was feeling upset.

I shook my head, feeling sorry for him.

'No, I'm afraid not, Ahmet. Now off you go,' said Mrs Sanders, patting Ahmet on the arm gently.

Ms Hemsi came to lead us out through the invisible clouds of smells. By now, most of the reporters were running out too. Some of them were even pushing past the classes in front of them to get out of the hall quicker.

As we left the stage and hurried out behind Ms Hemsi, I felt a tickle at the back of my neck. Sometimes you can tell right away when someone is staring at you – it's like an invisible hand giving the back of your head a push. Sometimes the push can be a friendly one, but most of the time the push is a surprising and scary one – especially when the stare contains a bad feeling like the one I was getting right then.

So I looked over my shoulder. As I did, my eyes bumped straight into the bright, shining blue eyes of Brendan-the-Bully and I knew right away by the big smirky shape of his lips that he had done it! He had let off all the stink bombs somehow and had got his revenge on Ahmet by spoiling our special Royal assembly. I didn't know how he had done it. He hadn't moved from his chair in the middle of our class row, and Chris and Liam had stayed next to him too, so he must have used something special to make the whole school stink. Maybe he had a super special remote control gadget – or had people to help him on the other side of the hall! However he had done it, I knew I had to find out what else he had planned, and stop him from doing anything to ruin our tea with the Queen.

THE INVISIBLE STINKS

For the rest of the day, the whole school and everyone in it smelled of farts mixed together with the stink of old dustbins. But the smell wasn't nearly as bad as seeing Ahmet go quiet and sad. Josie and Michael tried to cheer him up by saying that the assembly didn't matter, because the Queen was still going to be waiting for us, and Tom gave him a sticker of a famous footballer at lunch time, and I gave him all the lemon sherbets I had. But Ahmet still stayed quiet and sad which made us all feel quiet and sad too. It didn't help that the school stunk so bad that it felt as if we might never be able to smell anything normal or nice again.

Our librarian, Mrs Finnicky, was so disgusted

by the pong everyone was carrying with them that she closed the library for the whole day – she said it was because she didn't want any of her books to smell as badly as we did and that humans were easier to wash clean than paper pages. And Mrs Sanders did something that no one had ever heard of her doing in the whole history of the school: she cancelled every single one of her after-school detention sessions. She said having to smell like garbage all day was punishment enough for everyone, and that it was her duty to the planet to make sure we all got home as quickly as we could so that we could take a shower.

But the person I felt most sorry for was Mr Whittaker, the school cleaner, because thirteen people in the school were sick straight after the assembly. And as most of the people being sick were the teachers, he had a lot more cleaning up to do than if it had been just us kids throwing up. Usually no one ever saw Mr Whittaker, but on this day, I saw him at least twenty times, running up and down the corridors with a mop and bucket and muttering angrily at everyone who passed by him.

'Man,' said Tom, shaking his head as we all made our way out into the playground at home-time and heard a mop and bucket clanking past us. 'I think Mr Whittaker is going to need a holiday after today!'

'Yes,' said Ahmet. 'And new mop too!'

I grinned at Ahmet and gave him a thumbs up. Now that he was beginning to speak English more and we could understand him better, his jokes were getting funnier.

'I hope we don't still smell tomorrow when we go to see the Queen!' said Michael, waving his arms up and down in the air as if that would help make the stench go away. But it didn't. Instead it made him trip on his undone shoelaces. He would have fallen over, but Ahmet caught his arm and stopped him.

'Thanks, Ahmet,' said Michael, pushing up his glasses. Michael never thanks any of the rest of us when we stop him from banging into things or falling over. He only ever thanks Ahmet, and it always makes Ahmet shrug and Tom give an almost invisible scowl.

'I see you tomorrow, yes?' asked Ahmet, spotting his foster mum waving at him through the school gates. She was wearing the same long red woolly scarf that she always wore, and today her blonde hair was blowing around in the wind so much it looked like *it* was trying to be a scarf too.

'Yes,' I said. 'You are coming to my house tomorrow so that my Uncle Lenny can drive us to the Queen's!'

Ahmet nodded and, giving us all a wave, ran off to join his foster mum. We watched as he reached her and stood stiffly, like a soldier in an army, so that she could bend down to give him a hug. I guess he always stood like that because she wasn't his real mum and he was still waiting for his real mum to come and join him. His foster mum never seemed to care. She always hugged him and ruffled his hair anyway. But today, as she was hugging him, her usually smiling face began to frown.

'Ooooh, I think the stink's gone up her nose!'

whispered Tom. Ahmet's foster mum quickly stood up straight, and taking a step back, shook her head and made a funny noise with her throat – like a goose choking on a peanut.

'Someone should have warned her,' said Tom, shaking his head. 'As soon as I get home, I'm going to tell everyone to hold their breaths until I've had a shower. Especially Dad! He's got asthma! One sniff of me and it could finish him off!'

'Guys . . . what if we *do* still smell this bad tomorrow?' asked Josie. Grabbing her plait, she tried to pull it close to her nose so that she could smell it. 'Eugh!' she cried, wrinkling her freckles. 'It doesn't even reach and I can smell it! The Queen might throw up! And then she'd have us arrested!'

'Wait! Maybe THAT was his plan,' I exclaimed, giving Tom a punch on the arm. Tom rubbed the spot and looked at me, confused.

'What plan?' asked Tom. 'Whose plan?'

'You know,' I explained. 'Brendan-the-Bully's! He was the one who set off those stink bombs, I know he was. What if he stink-bombed the *whole* school not *just* to ruin the assembly, but so that we smelled so bad tomorrow that the Queen's guards would stop us from seeing her!'

Josie, Michael and Tom stopped and stared at me with their mouths open. After exactly two seconds, they all shook their heads.

'Nah! Brendan-the-Bully's not that clever!' said Tom.

'And we don't know for sure that it was him!' said Josie.

'I agree,' added Michael, frowning. 'We shouldn't think it was him right away just because we don't like him. Mum's always saying we shouldn't cloud our brains with bad judgements, or the wrong person gets blamed and put in jail. We have to see the evidence.'

Tom and Josie nodded in agreement, because Michael's mum was a lawyer who was always rescuing people and trying to make people's judgements act fair again.

I looked around the playground to see if Brendan-the-Bully was close by. Maybe if they could all see his smirky lips they would know

I wasn't being unfair. But I couldn't see him anywhere. Instead I saw Jenny, who ran the school newspaper – with a crowd gathering around her!

'Come on! There's Jenny,' I said, grabbing Josie's arm and dragging her after me. 'She might know more about what happened.'

We ran over and joined the whispering crowd standing in a circle around Jenny. As the school's news reporter, Jenny spies and listens and tells everyone everything about what's going on in school. The only problem is, she's not a very good reporter, because her stories often have lots of bits in them that aren't true. But because she mixes them up with things that *are* true, no one can tell the difference, except the person the story is about. Most people just believe her because it's easy and they don't have to think so hard about it.

'What's she saying?' asked Tom, leaning in.

A boy in front of us, who was from the year below, looked over and whispered, 'She says she knows who the stink bombers are! But she can't tell us their names because they're a part of a gang.'

'No waaaaaaaay,' whispered Josie, as Jenny began to speak even louder, so that everyone could hear her.

'Yeah! An *international* gang! And TODAY was the day they wanted everyone to know they're real!' shouted Jenny, grabbing her two long plaits and twisting and un-twisting them around her hands like smooth, brown snakes. 'There's one of them in EVERY school in the world now and that means every school is gonna get stink-bombed one day. But they picked OUR school first and they picked today because they knew the reporters were going to be here and because we're already famous because of that Ahmet kid!'

'What's the name of the gang?' asked someone, as we all huddled in closer.

'Yeah! And what's their symbol? Is it like a fart cloud?' shouted someone else.

'How come we've never heard of them before?' asked a girl standing in front of Michael.

Standing on her tiptoes, Jenny popped her head up above everyone else's like a submarine's eye to check for Eaves Droppers and enemy reporters who might steal her story, and then, crouching back down, whispered loudly, 'I'm not supposed to know this, but I'll tell you. The gang is called the Invisible Stinks and their mission is to make sure that everyone is—'

'What's happening here then?'

We all jumped away from Jenny as Mr Whittaker's large, balding head and brown uniform broke through the crowd and loomed over us.

'Anyone been sick? Because if they have, they can bleeding-buckets well clean it up themselves!'

Everyone stared up at Mr Whittaker in silence.

'Go on then, off with you! If you're not puking your guts out, you should be getting yourselves home and cleaned up so you smell human again!' And, waving us away, Mr Whittaker headed back into the school.

A car horn beeped across the air, making Jenny jump up and grab her bag. 'I'll tell you more on Monday!' she shouted as she ran over to her dad's car.

'But we can't wait until Monday!' said Tom grumpily to us, as the crowd broke up and we headed to the bus stop.

'The Invisible Stinks Gang could strike anywhere. What if they target the palace next?' asked Josie, walking faster and faster so that we would get to the bus stop before the next bus.

We boarded the bus home along with everyone else from school who needed to go in the same direction. After a minute or two, the grown-ups already on the bus started to frown, just like Ahmet's foster mum had done. Some of them held their noses shut with the tips of their fingers. Others shuffled in their seats and tutted loudly, trying to move their faces closer to the open windows. And after a few seconds, a dog began to howl. By the third stop, the whole bus was empty of anyone who wasn't from school.

'That was fun!' said Tom, as he jumped off at our stop. 'I think I might join the Invisible Stinks Gang if it means I can get a seat on the bus every day!'

'You do know that's not the name of a real gang, don't you?' I said, rolling my eyes. I couldn't believe that Tom had actually fallen for Jenny's story! 'Jenny was making that up. It was Brendan-the-Bully who did it. I know it was! It was him and Chris and Liam punishing Ahmet for nearly getting them expelled.'

'But they were all sitting together in assembly, remember?' Josie reminded me. 'And the stink bombs were coming from everywhere!'

'They got some other people to help,' I said. 'Other bullies in the school who don't like Ahmet.'

'But no one *saw* them do it,' said Michael, shrugging. 'Not even you. So you can't be sure!'

But I *was* sure. And I was going to prove it. All I needed was a little help from the Queen . . .

THE STORY THAT BROKE
THE INTERNET

The next morning, I jumped out of bed so hard my knees shook and the floorboards groaned. It was finally here! The day that me and my very best friends on the whole entire planet had been waiting for: we were going to go and meet the Queen! The real, live, *actual* Queen – the one that we saw on our pocket money and in the newspaper and on the television and on stamps.

And just as soon as I realised it was here and that I had to get ready, I instantly felt sick. It's funny how your brain can be so happy about something that it feels as if it might burst into a billion stars at any moment, but your body can feel like it has the flu and is hot and cold and sweaty and giddy. As if there are two different people stuck inside of you having a fight.

'Ah, you're up early!' said my mum, walking in with a huge smile on her face. Mum doesn't really smile very often – not properly – but when she does, it feels like magic and as if anything can happen.

Mum used to smile all the time when Dad was alive – even when there wasn't any real reason for her to smile. Like when Dad never read the signs properly and got lost driving us to an adventure and she had to read the maps properly for him, or when she had to eat another dinner that Dad had half-burned without meaning to. Dad loved cooking and driving but he was never good at them – even though he was a carpenter and could make whatever he wanted with his hands. I can remember Mum making fun of him and making him laugh too.

But four years ago, when I was six, Dad died in a car accident, which made Mum stop smiling. Now she only smiles when something extra-special happens. So I want to make as many extra-special things happen every day as I possibly can.

Some days it's hard. But other days are easier. Like the day you're about to go and have tea and biscuits and who knew what kind of cakes with the Queen.

Feeling too excited to do anything else, I ran and gave Mum a hug. But I was jumping up and down at the same time, so it wasn't as warm and cuddly as it should have been.

'Calm down, calm down!' laughed Mum, as she stroked my head. 'We can't have you hopping all over the place like a frog when you go to meet the Queen!' She gave my head a long sniff. 'And you smell fine now, thank goodness! Go and wash up and I'll get breakfast ready, OK? You've got hours yet!'

I nodded and, still jumping up and down because I was too excited not to, went and got as clean as I could. I had washed out the horrible smells from my hair and nose last night, but I wanted to make extra-sure I didn't smell even a little bit like stink bomb. So I scrubbed my face extra hard with soap and brushed my teeth for an extra minute and used three extra squirts of hand wash.

Then I ran back into my room and closed my door and stared up at the clothes Mum had hung up on a large hanger to make sure they wouldn't get creased. There was my most special black shirt with sparkling silver stars and golden planets all over it that Mum had ironed until it looked brand new – even though it wasn't and I had worn it to at least four parties and even to Buckingham Palace on my last adventure there. But the Queen hadn't seen it that last time because of everything that had gone wrong, so it didn't matter. Then behind my shirt was a brand-new pair of black jeans that Uncle Lenny had bought for me – because he said going to meet the Queen was like going to a wedding, and that you should always wear at least one new thing. And tucked into the pocket of the jeans was an extra-special pair of socks that I had bought with my own pocket money. They were bright blue with little dogs all over them – because I read that the Queen likes dogs, and if I run out of things to say to her or if she starts to look sleepy and bored, I can show her my socks. It's good to have a back-up plan.

I was in such a rush to get dressed that I banged my arm on the door and stubbed my toe on the bed, but I was too happy and excited to feel any pain. I was pulling on my second sock when I heard the doorbell ring and Mum running to open it.

'There's my little tiger!' cried Uncle Lenny, as I ran out of my room to see who it was. Uncle Lenny is Mum's brother. He has a moustache that tickles my face whenever he gives me a kiss on the cheek, and, because he's a taxi driver, he likes putting his hands on my shoulders and pushing me around the flat as if I was a car. I was so glad that my horrible Aunt Christina wasn't with him that I gave him a running hug too. Aunt Christina isn't nearly as nice as Uncle Lenny – no matter what's happening or how happy you might be, she always looks confused and angry at the same time, and sniffs the air as if her nose is hunting for clues.

'All spruced up and ready to go, I see!' said Uncle Lenny, holding me away with his arms extra straight so that he could see all of me at the same time. 'You look as if you're fit to go see a Queen! Oh, wait a minute! You are!' Uncle Lenny looked at me for a second and then began to laugh so much that a tear fell out of his eye. Then, shaking his head, he muttered, 'Ah! That was a good one!'

Grown-ups always like laughing at the things they say – even when what they're saying doesn't seem even a bit funny. It's very strange, but then, most grown-ups are. Even Uncle Lenny sometimes.

Mum brought me a bowl of porridge with a small mountain of strawberry jam in the middle and Uncle Lenny switched on the telly. Usually I wasn't allowed to have breakfast on the sofa and watch telly too, but it was such a special day that it felt like all the normal rules didn't matter any more.

'Here, look,' said Uncle Lenny, putting the volume up. 'Your school's on the news again! I saw it last night too.'

'Really?' I asked, feeling surprised. Mum had worked late at the library last night and Mrs Abbey, our next-door neighbour who looks after me sometimes, had wanted to watch a programme about people who tried to bake perfect cakes and then cried when they couldn't. So I had spent all evening reading my favourite Tintin comic books instead, and thinking about the different cakes the Queen might be asking her bakers to make for us, and how I could convince her to help me prove that Brendan-the-Bully was a Stinking Criminal. I didn't think reporters would care about Ahmet and the assembly because it was cancelled, so I hadn't watched the news at all.

As I took a bite of my porridge and Mum took a bite of her toast and Uncle Lenny took a sip of his coffee, the newsreader on the TV looked out at us with a serious look on her face. Behind her was a picture of my school hall – it showed everyone frozen right in the middle of running and screaming and looking extra panicky.

'Newham's Nelson School is once again at the centre of a scandal that is rocking the nation,' said the newsreader.

'What? Because of the *stink bombs*?' I asked, wondering how stink bombs in an assembly could rock a whole nation.

'Shhhhh,' said Mum, putting down her toast.

Mum only ever put food back down on her plate when she was serious or angry, so I put down my spoonful of porridge too.

The newsreader, as if she had been waiting for us to be quiet, continued. 'Yesterday, stink bombs disrupted the school as it gathered for a morning assembly, leading some to wonder if the act was a protest against the impending meeting between Her Majesty the Queen and Ahmet, the refugee boy who made headlines a few weeks ago.'

'It wasn't a protest against that!' I cried, feeling angry. 'It was just Brendan-the-Bully being stupid!'

'Shhhhhhhhhhhhhhhh!' ordered Mum again, leaning closer in towards the telly.

'Ahmet was made famous for inspiring a group of children from his class to attempt a break-in at Buckingham Palace. Their aim was simple: to obtain the Queen's help with locating his family – an act which sparked headlines and inspired the Queen to invite Ahmet to tea. In a special address to his school, Ahmet was due to give details about his forthcoming visit, but was cut short by a flurry of stink bombs, leading to a mass evacuation of the premises and many children and teachers falling ill. Now, it seems that what was thought to be merely a childish prank, may have actually been part of a wider protest taking place on streets of London. Here is Ramesh Djai with the full story.'

The picture on the television changed from the newsreader to a video of our school hall. I could see Ahmet and me and Josie and Tom and Michael, all standing on the stage, looking very small and Ahmet's mouth moving, and then a puff of grey-green smoke and everyone running and screaming and pushing each other away.

But the screams were silent, because over the video there was a man's voice saying: 'Yesterday morning, hundreds of pupils were forced to flee from the assembly hall at Nelson School, after a coordinated stink bomb attack. Caught on film by the press, videos of the event are now going viral. The scene was one of pandemonium and chaos, with many asking: was this a protest staged by students who disagree with the presence of refugee children at their school?'

The video of school was paused, and the picture changed again, this time to a tall, grey-haired man standing in the middle of a long, red road. I recognised the road right away – it was the exact same road me and Tom had walked down a few weeks ago to get help for Ahmet and his family!

'I'm here this bright Saturday morning in front of Buckingham Palace, where in just a few short hours, the Queen is due to meet with a child who might be the most famous refugee on the planet – a boy we all know as "Ahmet".' The reporter frowned as if the name 'Ahmet' was so serious it deserved a special frown of its own. The frown went deeper as he said, 'It's a meeting that has sparked endless debates, with some saying the Queen is overstepping her neutral position as head of state by welcoming a refugee of war to tea, and others arguing that supporting refugee children and families falls within the confines of her role.'

The camera suddenly pulled away and turned left from the reporter's face. Right behind him, you could see a group of people holding up large signs and shouting angrily. Their signs said things like 'Immigrants Not Wanted' and 'Go Back to Where You Belong!' and 'Refugees Not Welcome'. Lots of them were wearing big blue stickers that said, 'Fry for Prime Minister!'.

But opposite them, on the other side of the road, was another group of people with signs that said 'Refugees Welcome' and 'For Queen and All Countries' and 'All Ahmets Welcome!'.

The camera went back to the reporter. Only now the reporter wasn't alone any more. There was a man standing next to him. A man with large black eyes and a dark grey suit and a bright blue tie. He was someone I had seen before and who Mum hated so much that seeing him now made her slam down her plate on the coffee table with an angry bang.

Uncle Lenny looked down at me and gave me a wink, which instantly made me feel less scared.

'Joining me now is Member of Parliament and leader of the National Union of Great Britannia party, Mr John Fry,' said the news reporter, holding out a microphone. 'MP Fry, what do you make of the anger being directed at what is, to all ends, just an innocent tea party between the Queen of England and a ten-year-old boy?'

Mr Fry smiled and looked at the camera, which made Mum make an angry growling noise with her throat.

'Innocent?' he asked. 'Manipulating our monarchy for political ends is anything but innocent. Refugees leave their countries to take things that aren't theirs to take – whether that's jobs or homes or places in our schools or space in our hospitals. And, were I Prime Minister, I would have advised the Queen against meeting with these five highly dangerous children.'

'Dangerous?' asked the reporter. He looked at the camera and then at the MP as if he was beginning to feel uncomfortable. 'Surely you can't view these children as dangerous?'

'Yes. Dangerous. Any group of children willing to break the rules and attack the Royal Guards as these children had planned to do just a few weeks ago, are *highly* dangerous. And I am not the only one who thinks so. The protesters who let off the stink bombs in these children's school yesterday clearly feel the same – the whole thing STINKS. Refugees should NOT be—'

'That's quite enough!' said Mum, picking up the remote control and turning off the television.

'Couldn't agree with you more,' said Uncle Lenny. Then, giving me a nudge with his arm, he said, 'We don't need no small *fry* ruining our day with the Queen now, do we?' And, laughing again, he wiped another tear away, as I stared and wondered what was so funny this time.

I glanced over at Mum, who was looking at Uncle Lenny too and shaking her head and grinning. I wanted to ask her at least five questions about how we were going to get to the palace when there were so many people there and what if the Queen got upset and didn't want to see us any more, but just then the buzzer to our flat rang. Mum jumped up and pressed the special camera button, then cried out, 'Come on up, Josie!'

Over the next hour, our flat went from just having me and Mum and Uncle Lenny in it to having: me and Mum and Uncle Lenny; Josie and her mum and dad; Michael and his mum and dad; Tom and his mum; and Ahmet and his foster mum. Which, for a very small flat, was quite a lot of people and quite a lot of noise!

But everyone was so happy and looked so nice that it didn't seem to matter that no one could sit down. Everyone had worn their very best outfits: Ahmet was wearing a bright blue suit and a white shirt and a bow tie with dots on it and he had his red rucksack with him; Josie was wearing a pair of sparkly dungarees over a long-sleeve white top that had tiny yellow crowns all over it and a brand-new pair of football trainers; Michael was wearing trousers that he said were made of tartan from Scotland, and a white shirt with a tie that matched his trousers; Tom was wearing a waistcoat that shined blue and green at the same time, and a dark blue T-shirt that had a picture of a Lego Queen. I think he had put extra gel in his hair today too because it looked stiffer and more golden-yellow than it normally did.

Mum and me had spent all of last night cleaning and tidying and polishing and putting our books straight to make the flat nice for everyone, instead of watching a film or reading an extra-long story together like we normally did on Friday nights. I was glad it looked so nice, and I was especially glad I had tidied up my room, because it was the first time Ahmet and Michael and Tom had seen it.

I mostly only have books in my room and a table filled with some of Dad's old pens and tools, but the one super-cool thing I have is the old-fashioned record player Dad left me. I played a record on it for everyone, and for the first time in a long time, it didn't seem to make Mum sad. I think she knew Dad would have liked everyone listening to one of his songs together.

'It's eleven o'clock, kids. Time to go!' announced Uncle Lenny, opening the front door and standing beside it like a butler. 'Won't do to be late for the Queen, and traffic is never a friend to anyone on a Saturday!'

I looked around at my friends and gave them a massive grin. It was finally time to go and see the Queen and ask her our Most Important Questions! And no one – not Mr MP Fry, or the people with the angry faces and signs, or Brendan-the-Bully's stink bombs or even videos that were breaking the internet – could stop us.

5

MISSED DIRECTIONS

'In you hop!' said Uncle Lenny, opening the back door to his shiny, black cab. I love Uncle Lenny's cab because it feels like a mini limousine – it looks small on the outside but has enough space to fit seven people inside it – and at least five suitcases too. And it has lots of buttons and windows and slots and lights as well, so at night it feels like a spaceship. I could tell right away that it had been cleaned especially for today, because it smelled like cleaning polish.

'This is first time!' Ahmet smiled, as he jumped into the cab behind me. 'In home, taxis they are white!'

I suddenly wondered what taxis in different countries of the world looked like, and if they were all like mini limousines too.

'Are you sure you don't want me to come?' asked Mum, patting my hair and smoothening my shirt for the tenth time.

I nodded. I secretly wished the Queen had invited all our parents and Ahmet's foster mum and Ms Hemsi and maybe even Mrs Khan to tea too, but she hadn't. Instead, she had said there were going to be two special guards to meet us at the entry door, and that whoever was with us could wait in a waiting room. I didn't want Mum to come to the palace and not be able to go in with me. It would feel worse than it did saying bye to her from outside our home. So we both agreed she would stay behind.

'DON'T SPEAK UNLESS YOU'RE SPOKEN TO, DARLING!' shouted Tom's mum, as she shut the door after us. She gestured to Uncle Lenny to buzz down the window, and continued, 'REMEMBER! SHE'S THE QUEEN OF ENGLAND! NOT YOUR AUNT MACY!'

'Michael? Michael! REMEMBER! Do NOT ask the Queen about how you can access the MI6 building!' cried Michael's dad.

'Ahmet – don't make the Queen smell the rucksack, OK, darling?' said Ahmet's foster mum, waving. 'Just show it to her.'

'Remember to have fun, kids!' Josie's dad smiled.

Her mum started to cry, muttering, 'Can't believe my baby's off to see the Queen! Never in all me life!'

I looked at Mum and waited for her to say something. But she just pushed up her glasses and gave me a wink. As if to tell me that no matter what I did, she would be waiting to hear all about it when I got home. The wink made me miss my dad and made my nose tickle, so I winked back with both my eyes, one after the other.

'Seatbelts on?' asked Uncle Lenny.

We all gave him thumbs up.

'Good, good! Then off we go!'

As we swerved away from the pavement and waved bye to our mums and dads, Michael, whose seat was facing the back, twisted around towards Uncle Lenny's special glass window and shouted, 'MR LENNY SIR, CAN YOU PUT THE METER ON?'

'Michael, mate, you don't need to shout!' said Uncle Lenny, laughing. And then looking into his special mirror, he frowned at us through his reflection and asked, 'Why do you want the meter on?'

Michael shrugged and said, 'So I can watch the numbers go up and see how much money it would have cost if we were paying.'

Uncle Lenny laughed again, and, tipping his cap, he said, 'Aye aye, Captain!', and switched on his money box. That's the box that every taxi has that counts how much a driver is owed. In most taxis the numbers are red, but I told my Uncle Lenny that it looked scary – like the numbers that you saw on bombs in big action movies – so he managed to change the colours for his box to yellow.

Michael watched for a moment until the numbers changed from £2.50 to £3.00. Then he gave a big sigh and smiled, looking happier than I had ever seen him.

Taking a journey in a black taxi from one part of London to another is fun when you're on your own. But when you're with your very best friends, wearing your most favourite clothes, and the driver happens to be the greatest uncle ever, it feels like the most exciting journey in the world. Even the boring parts of the city that you see every day change shape and become shiny and new – as if they secretly belong to a brand-new city that you can only ever see when you're sitting behind a different window. We all giggled and pointed and poked each other in the arm as Uncle Lenny drove us past houses that got bigger and redder and taller, and shops that shone with more and more lights. The numbers on Uncle Lenny's meter got higher and higher until it reached exactly £52.40, and the cab slowed down and came to a stop.

'Hold up . . . what do we have here, then?' asked Uncle Lenny, looking around.

I looked out of our window and shook Tom's knee. I knew where we were! We were near the palace! Up ahead were the huge arches crossing the large red road that we had walked through just two weeks ago – when we had been on a completely different and far scarier adventure.

Someone tapped on Uncle Lenny's window. We all leaned over to see who it was. It was a police officer with a helmet on her head and dark brown eyes.

'Sorry, sir, but you won't be able to turn here,' she said, pointing in the direction of a long line of police who were standing across the road. 'There's a protest so the road is blocked.'

'This is like the last time!' whispered Tom, looking worried.

'I see that,' said Uncle Lenny. 'But these children here have an appointment with the Queen.'

The police officer tilted her head to one side. 'Have they now?' she asked.

We all nodded as Ahmet pulled out his invitation to show her. Pushing it to Uncle Lenny through the slot where people usually put their money, he said, 'It is real – from the real Queen!'

Uncle Lenny handed the police officer the invitation. She read it, smiling a little bit.

This is what Ahmet's invitation looked like:

The Lord Chamberlain is commanded by Her Majesty

to invite

Ahmet Saggal,

The Bravest Refugee Boy I Know

to a Special Afternoon Tea

at Buckingham Palace

on Saturday, 27th October at 12 noon.

THIS CARD DOES NOT GUARANTEE ADMITTANCE.

'They're meant to be at the East Gate in ten minutes,' explained Uncle Lenny, looking at his watch nervously.

The police officer nodded and, turning away from us, started speaking into the walkie-talkie that was taped to her bright yellow police jacket.

'What if they don't let us go through in time?' whispered Josie. Grabbing the end of the plait her mum and dad had made her put her hair into again, she tried pulling it to her mouth.

60

'Here you go,' said the police officer, poking her head through the window and giving Ahmet back his invitation. 'You can head on down to the East Gate – but you're going to have to leave the cab here, I'm afraid. The crowds are a little too thick for a vehicle to get through, so instead, Officer Jensen and Officer Wu will be escorting you.' She pointed over her shoulder to two officers in bright yellow jackets and waved at them to join us.

'All right,' said Uncle Lenny. 'Where shall I park up?'

'Just leave the vehicle here,' said the police officer, pointing to a spot right beside her. 'And Mr Ahmet Saqqal?'

We all looked at Ahmet, as Ahmet looked up at the police officer.

'It's a pleasure to have met you.' And, with a tap of her helmet, she smiled and waved us through the long line of officers standing behind her like a human wall.

Ahmet went bright red and, smiling with all of his face, put his invitation carefully away again in his rucksack.

'Come on, kids, we best hurry!' said Uncle Lenny, as he parked the cab and Officers Jensen and Wu joined us. Officer Jensen was very tall and pale and almost had as many freckles as Josie, and Officer Wu was skinny with shiny black hair, and had a frown that was as deep as a miniature ditch on his forehead.

'Right, kids, looks like we might have to run!' said Officer Jensen as Uncle Lenny swung open the car door and grabbed my hand. I jumped out and everyone else leaped out behind me.

'Join hands and don't let go,' instructed Officer Wu, walking in front of us. 'Follow me, please!'

We all joined hands and began to walk as fast as we could down the large red road towards the palace, looking like a short and bobbing snake. Both Officers Wu and Jensen kept on waving at us from the front, as they shouted, 'Make way, please, make way!' to the crowds around us.

But as we got closer and closer to the large black gates of the palace and the huge water fountain that lay in the middle of the road, it got harder and harder to see Officer Jensen – even though he was so tall, or to hear Officer Wu. There were so many other police officers everywhere and so many people with cameras and bags and prams and cards, and so much noise, that we kept on having to let go of each other's hands and quickly join up again to make it through the crowd. But then, even that got harder to do too.

'Try to keep up!' cried out Officer Wu, as Uncle Lenny let go of my hand and waved at us to walk closely in a line behind him instead. But the crowds were getting taller and squashier and louder, and within a few seconds, I couldn't see the top of Uncle Lenny's head any more or Officer Jensen's helmet or Officer Wu's bright jacket. All I could see were people's coats and trousers and shoes. And all I could hear were people shouting about refugees and how they were welcome and how they weren't.

I looked behind me to make sure that everyone was still there, but all I could see was Michael pushing up his glasses and struggling to keep up with me. I turned around to tell Uncle Lenny to ask the officers to slow down – but he was gone!

That was when I heard someone shout, 'LOOK! IT'S HIM! IT'S THAT REFUGEE KID, AHMET!'

Instantly, everyone around us turned to look and shout and point. I stopped and hopped around to try and see where Ahmet was to make sure he was OK. Michael joined me and then so did Josie and Tom – but we couldn't see Ahmet anywhere.

And just then someone else shouted, 'HERE! THOSE ARE HIS FRIENDS!'

The crowd around us shuffled and pointed and stared at us, as cameras clicked, and my breath began to feel squashed. Some of the faces around us were frowning and angry and they were holding up the horrible signs I had seen on the news. They got closer and closer, pinning us into the middle of a circle, when suddenly, Josie gasped. I looked over my shoulder in the direction she was staring and saw what had made her go so white.

Through a small gap in the crowd, I could see Ahmet, who was standing about ten steps away. He was nearly surrounded by another crowd. But he wasn't alone. He was staring up at a man, and the man was holding Ahmet's red rucksack, as if he was trying to stop him from running away. I knew right away who the man was by his dark blue suit and the golden ring he was wearing on his little finger. It was MP Fry!

But it wasn't seeing him that made me suddenly feel as if my hands and feet had frozen. It was seeing the man next to him. A man with a long face and long nose and long lips and a large brown bristly moustache . . .

It was Mr Irons – the strictest, most horrible, most hated teacher who had ever taught at our school.

Michael and Tom had seen him at the same time. They gasped as Josie cried out, 'What's HE doing here?'

We all stared at Mr Irons. He had helped Brendan-the-Bully get away with hurting Ahmet! And now he was here, smiling down at Ahmet as if he had just been given the world's best birthday present, and making my insides feel like jelly and fire all at the same time.

And without thinking or being ready or knowing what I was doing, I felt my legs push against the ground, and my arms push everyone around me away and my voice cry out, 'YOU LEAVE HIM ALONE!' and for a few seconds, everything seemed to stop.

I had reached Ahmet and MP Fry and Mr Irons, and heard the footsteps and breaths of Tom and Josie and Michael as they came up behind me. I reached out and touched Ahmet's arm, so that he knew I was there with him. My heart was marching through my head and my stomach felt like it was an ocean full of crashing waves, but I didn't care. We stood and stared up at MP Fry and Mr Irons and all the people around them who were staring back at us, and waited for whatever was about to happen next.

But as we waited, from somewhere in the distance, a clock struck twelve. Something heavy dropped into the ocean in my stomach and sank to the very bottom. Because I knew right away that we weren't ever going to get to the Queen on time, or get to ask her our Ten Most Important Questions.

THE LORD OF CHAMBERS
AND LIONS

Sometimes, the quietest people can surprise you –
especially when they get angry.

I knew that because I had seen Ahmet fight
bullies when he had never even spoken two words
in English, and I had seen Mum yell at a man
who was being horrible to a woman on the bus,
when she never usually yells and instead tries to
'bite her tongue'. I can't bite my tongue because
it hurts too much, so I always say what I think
most times. So do Tom and Josie. But Michael
never says anything when he gets angry or upset
– he goes quiet and looks if he's thinking a Deep
Thought or waiting for someone else to speak up
for him.

So, standing there in front of MP Fry, who was

still holding on to Ahmet's bag, nobody expected Michael to say the things he said. In fact, I don't think even Michael expected it, because his face looked so surprised and confused afterwards.

This is what Michael shouted: 'YOU GIVE AHMET HIS BAG BACK, OR I'M GOING TO FIGHT YOU AND SUE YOU AND MY MUM WILL TAKE YOU TO COURT FOR BEING A – A BAG-SNATCHER WHO SNATCHES BAGS FROM REFUGEE CHILDREN! SO GIVE IT BACK NOW OR ELSE!'

When he had finished, I could feel Michael shaking next to me and I heard Tom whispering, 'Woah!'

Then, from somewhere in the crowd on the other side of the road, a man shouted, 'YEAH! YOU GO MY LAD!' and a woman cried out, 'SHAME ON YOU, FRY! SHAME ON YOU, FRY!' And within a few seconds, lots of people were shouting out the exact same thing as the woman. I looked across the road to where they were all standing and saw the nicer signs that I had seen on the news that morning. I realised that we had been trying to push through the horrible crowd to get to the Queen's palace, when we should have gone through the opposite side!

That was when I saw Uncle Lenny and Officer Jensen and Officer Wu pushing their way through the crowd towards us, looking red and sweaty and hot. Officer Wu was shouting something into the large walkie-talkie on his shoulder that sounded like 'Back-up! Back-up! Centre point 312!'

'Are you all OK?' panted Uncle Lenny, quickly checking our faces with his eyes.

I didn't answer, because MP Fry had grabbed Ahmet's bag and was raising it up in the air. It was clear he wanted to say something. Uncle Lenny stood behind us with his hands on mine and Ahmet's shoulders. It felt as if he was our bodyguard and as if nothing in the world could ever hurt us. The crowds slowly became quiet as the police officers and the cameras and reporters pushed closer, making MP Fry's smile wider. I didn't like seeing Ahmet's red rucksack in MP Fry's hands, because I knew how important it was to Ahmet, and how badly he had wanted to show it to the Queen. But I made myself stay still and wait, because I knew I was too short to reach it.

As MP Fry began to speak, half of the crowd began to boo and hiss whilst the other half cried out, 'Darn right!' There was a pounding in my ears, just like a drum beating, so I couldn't hear any of his words except 'Queen and country' and 'duty'.

All around us the crowds seemed to be getting bigger and taller, so I held on tighter to Ahmet's arm. I could tell he was getting angry because he beginning to stand more stiffly and his hands were curling up into fists – just like they had done when he had roared at Brendan-the-Bully in the playground once. But I knew we were safe because now a lot of other police officers had joined Officer Jensen and Officer Wu, and all of them were busy trying to make the crowds stay back and not squash us.

I looked up at Mr Irons and saw he was still smiling at us, as if seeing Ahmet upset made him happy. MP Fry was smiling too, so much that it was as if his teeth had taken over most of his face. He was waving at the people behind us, and looking at the news cameras.

Then, suddenly, he raised his hands a second time. The booing and hissing and cheering instantly became quiet again as he took a step back and cried out, 'But don't just take my word for it! Mr Irons has first-hand experience of just how dangerous allowing refugees into our country and our schools can be!'

I felt my own mouth fall open as Mr Irons stepped proudly forward and took Ahmet's bag in his hands. I could hear Ahmet growling like an angry lion and felt Josie taking a step forwards as if she wanted to kick Mr Irons in the leg just as hard as she could. Everyone around us was now looking at Mr Irons, waiting to hear what he was going to say.

Mr Irons puffed up his chest and, stroking his moustache, looked at the cameras. He had just opened his mouth, when suddenly—

SCREEEEEEEEEEEEEEEEEEEEEEEEEEEEECH!

Everyone jumped and turned as the largest two gates of the palace began to slowly squeak open.

A hush fell over the crowd as all of the cameras and reporters and crowds turned away from Mr Irons towards the gates to see what was happening. After a few seconds, the gates clanged to a stop, and two of the Queen's special guards with their large pointy swords and giant black hats marched from their huts at the front of the palace right up to the corner of each gate, and gave a salute.

As soon as their fingers had touched their hats, two police officers on motorcycles appeared from the back of the palace, followed by a large black shiny car with two flags fluttering on the front bonnet. The flags were golden yellow and red and blue, and showed dancing lions and a harp.

Almost immediately, whispers and shouts began to fill the air.

'It's the Queen!'

'It's her butler!'

'It's the royal baby!'

'Quick! Take as many photos as you can!'

'Make sure you're rolling!'

The police officers in yellow jackets began to wave the crowds back against the walls so that the car could come through the palace gates and out on to the road. Even MP Fry and Mr Irons were forced to move to the side next to the Queen's large water fountain.

I looked at the car and its dark windows and wondered if the Queen had become so angry with us for missing tea and making people argue outside her house that we had made her leave the country. I wished I could have made her understand that it wasn't our fault, and that we had tried our best to get to her on time.

We watched as the car slowly rolled out of the gates and then headed towards the fountain. But instead of passing it by and continuing up the red road, it stopped. Right in front of us!

Ahmet grabbed my elbow and I grabbed Michael's, as a door swung open. Everyone gasped, as we waited to see who it was, hoping it would be the Queen.

But it wasn't. It was a man. A very tall, tanned man with brown and white hair, dressed in a black suit and wearing the largest golden necklace I had ever seen anyone wear in real life. He looked like he could be a mayor, but I knew the Mayor of London was a woman named Piya Muqit and I had seen what she looked like in the newspapers, so I knew it wasn't her.

Looking down at me and Ahmet and Tom and Josie and Michael, and bowing his head at Uncle Lenny, the man smiled and said, 'I hear you are running slightly late for your scheduled meeting with the Queen?'

Josie nodded and opened her mouth. But instead of saying 'Yes', she gave a hiccup so loud it seemed to echo across all of London. It made her turn so red that even her freckles seemed to disappear.

'Let me introduce myself. I am the Lord Chamberlain, and—'

'Woah! You mean you're the man who sent us our invitations?' interrupted Tom.

The Lord Chamberlain smiled again. 'And you must be Tom?'

Tom cried out 'Woah!' again and looked at me. He poked Michael on the arm as if Michael might not have heard and whispered, 'He knows my name!'

'And you must be Josie . . . and Michael . . . and Ahmet . . .' Holding out his hand to each of them in turn, he shook theirs. Then he turned to me and introduced himself to me and Uncle Lenny too and gave us a handshake that was as warm and as soft as a slice of freshly baked bread.

'As the Lord Chamberlain, I am responsible for overseeing all of Her Majesty's ceremonial duties – which includes looking after the very special guests permitted entrance on to her grounds and chambers. The Queen has taken note of the cause for your delay, and has sent me to fetch you – if you would kindly permit me to do so?'

'You mean . . . we get to go in your car?' asked Michael, so excited that he was pushing up his glasses even though they didn't have anywhere left to go.

The Lord Chamberlain smiled and, stepping back behind the door, waited for us all to climb in.

'We are going to meet Queen, yes?' asked Ahmet, squeezing my elbow even harder.

I was too excited for words to come out, so

instead I nodded as fast as I could.

'Good,' said Ahmet, as he turned around and took three steps up to Mr Irons. Putting his hands on his hips, he shouted, 'You give bag back to me! The Queen – she needs to see it. It is come all the way from Syria and is gift from my dad!'

With his face crumpled like a sulking baby's, Mr Irons slowly reached out, and gave Ahmet his red rucksack back. His nose began to whistle loudly and angrily like a very faraway train and some people behind him begin to mutter and whisper. But as soon as Ahmet had his bag back in his hands, a deafening cheer rippled through the crowd. I waited for the boos and hisses too, but there were none. The Lord Chamberlain had made them go silent.

Then, just as we were about to climb in the car, the Lord Chamberlain turned to MP Fry and, in a voice that was different and stricter to the one he had used for us, said, 'Her Majesty wishes to convey a message to you, sir.'

MP Fry stood up straight and held his nose high in the air – almost as high as Mr Irons'.

'Yes?' he asked.

The Lord Chamberlain continued, his voice very loud and clear, 'Her Majesty wishes to thank you for your concern regarding her position as the Head of State; but she would like me to remind you that she has been in this honoured position for longer than you have been alive. And, as the longest reigning monarch in history, she would also like to remind you of the depth and breadth of her knowledge as regards her duties and limitations.'

MP Fry looked as if he didn't know what to say, and, behind him, reporters and cameramen and lots of people in the crowd giggled and whispered. And then, as if his teeth were trying to stop his words from coming out, he replied, 'Please thank Her Majesty for her kind reminder.'

The Lord Chamberlain smiled and, after making sure we were all seated safely in the car, calmly walked around to the front seat to sit next to the driver.

'I THINK MP Fry just got TOLD!' whispered Tom, as the large black car turned smoothly back towards the palace, and another cheer rang through the air around us.

I grinned and felt Uncle Lenny give my hand a squeeze, as the flags with the golden lions and the Lord who looked after them led us towards all the Queen's grounds and chambers.

7

THE STATE AND ITS SECRETS

Meeting the Queen and eating finger sandwiches the size of really tiny fingers and thirteen different kinds of mini-cakes, and getting to ask her all the questions we wanted to ask, and playing with her dogs, and holding the crown she likes to wear best because it's the lightest and doesn't give her a Head Ache, made all of us so happy that I don't think we'll ever not be happy ever again. Even Uncle Lenny, who was allowed to meet the Queen for twenty whole seconds before being given tea and cake in her waiting room, said he had never known a day like it, and that it would stay with him for the rest of his life.

I think as happy as she made us, we made the Queen happy too, because after Ahmet showed her his bag and we all helped explain why it was so important, and he had asked her his questions about wars and handbags, and we had all asked our last question about how she could help other children like Ahmet too, she said she had never been asked questions like them before, and that she was proud of us for being brave enough to ask them.

But she also told us that everything she said in the palace was 'off the record' – which meant that everything she said needed to stay a secret. Even if it was something as small as knowing what her favourite fruit was! I guess it's because the Queen doesn't want anyone to record what she's saying in her own house, as it's where she has to do all of her State work and her Home work too. So when we got back to school and Mrs Sanders told us we were going to do another special assembly so that we could tell everyone about our visit – to make up for the one that had been stink-bombed – we didn't have anything new to say! We couldn't tell anyone what her answers to our Ten Most Important Questions were, or what her dogs' names were, or what cake she liked to eat best, or if she wore a wig or not, or if she liked the picture on the money and coins we used – even though we knew the answers now. All we were allowed to talk about was what we had worn and what food we had eaten and how many different cups of tea we had, and how many times I sneezed because I had forgotten I was allergic to dogs – even the Queen's ones. And about how much Ahmet had loved telling the Queen about his bag and his mum and dad and sister Syrah – and how the Queen hadn't minded smelling the bag at all! After that second assembly, Ahmet was still famous, but I think his red rucksack became even more famous, because now that everyone knew the Queen had smelled it, they wanted to smell it too.

And even though I couldn't share any of the Queen's secrets with Mum or Uncle Lenny, they didn't mind, because they got to share in all the things that happened straight after!

Things like MP Fry being forced to resign the very next week! And all because some people with whips in his party said that they didn't like how he had treated Ahmet and his red bag, and how he had insulted the Queen. I didn't know people in Parliament carried whips with them, but I guess that's why so many of them have briefcases. And I guess once you've been whipped, you can't go back, because MP Fry was never heard from again.

That same week, Mr Irons also tried to tell his story on the news, about how Ahmet was the one to blame for all the changes at our school, and how he was costing the school money because he needed extra help from people like Ms Hemsi. Mr Irons even tried to say he had lost his job because of these things and that Ahmet was to blame for everything that had happened to him. But then the reporters talked to parents from the school and found out the truth about why he didn't have a job any more, and how he had been a bad teacher, and after just two interviews, he disappeared too. I hope we never have to see him or his moustache or hear his whistling nose ever again!

And the very next week after that, my guess that Brendan-the-Bully was behind the stink bomb attacks was proven right! Well, nearly right.

Because there had been lots and lots of videos taken by the World's Press at the school on the day of our first assembly, someone had found one that showed who had set all the stink bombs off. Brendan-the-Bully, Liam, Chris and six other students were all caught! But even though the cameras had caught them, no one could figure out who was the leader, so instead of one person being punished, they all got a month's detention, and were never allowed into assembly again without having their pockets checked in front of everyone. I still know deep down that Brendan-the-Bully was the leader, because none of the other bullies cared about hurting Ahmet as much as he did. But he hasn't come after Ahmet or any of the rest of us since.

I was glad because I had asked the Queen to help me find proof, and I knew that she would. I guess she must have asked her special guards and officers to make the World's Press check their cameras again, otherwise Brendan-the-Bully might never have been caught.

And something else happened because of the

day we met the Queen. Something that feels more important than anything else – even us knowing secret secrets! And that's the Very Big Debate that is happening in Parliament right now! Every day, for two whole weeks, Mum has been bringing the newspaper home and letting me stay up late to watch the news on TV and try to understand it all. And at school, me and Josie and Tom and Michael and Ahmet have been asking Mrs Khan and Ms Hemsi to help us learn about it too.

The Very Big Debate is a word-fight – like the one we saw outside the palace. Except this one is between MPs and doesn't involve any signs. MPs are debating to see if they can keep the border gates open so that the whole country can help refugee children like Ahmet stay safe from wars and be with their families. I don't know what's going to happen, but now I know that some of the most powerful people in the country care and want to help, and Mum says that's a good start.

Mum also says that the Queen isn't the one who made the Very Big Debate happen, because she's not allowed to tell MPs what to talk about or what to do. But I don't think Queens and Kings always need to *tell* people what to say or do to show that they care.

Sometimes they can show that they care in other ways.

Like by posting a very special handwritten invitation. Or by sending a car with lion flags to come and rescue you when angry people are shouting. Or by hosting a tea party in their palace, where they give you finger sandwiches the size of really tiny fingers and thirteen different kinds of mini-cakes, and they tell you and your best friends all of the State's Secrets, and also let you show them your socks.

THE END

Onjali Q. Raúf is the founder of Making Herstory, an organisation which encourages men, women and children to work together to create a fairer and more equal world for women and girls everywhere. Her debut novel, *The Boy at the Back of the Class*, was the winner of the Blue Peter Book Award and the Waterstone's Children's Book Prize. *The Star Outside My Window* is her second book.

You can find her @OnjaliRauf on Twitter.

ALSO BY ONJALI Q. RAÚF

Read on for an extract of
Swimming Against the Storm,
Jess Butterworth's exciting new
adventure novel . . .

'We're here.' Avery jumps back down the other side of the tree trunk.

I pull myself up on the trunk and my shorts snag on a branch.

The trunk has been strangled by ivy.

The third lesson: Never Touch Poison Ivy.

I pause. It's too late. There's already a rash on my arm, red and raised. I fight the urge to scratch it.

I let myself gently thud down the other side of

the trunk. I notice the base of the stump and the hundreds of rings in it. The tree must have been hundreds of years old.

Avery's a few feet ahead, crouched low to the ground, pointing.

I bend over next to her. It's a footprint.

But not a normal one. It's giant. Four times the size of my foot. The print is sunk deep into the mud. Whatever made it must be heavy.

A crumpled leaf covers the base and I lift it up. The print has a human shape and five toes.

I kneel down next to it. It's huge but it looks like it came from a human. A giant human.

'Loup-garou,' whispers Avery, and as she says the words her eyes shine with excitement.

My stomach fills with butterflies. 'They can't be real,' I say under my breath.

Avery points to the ground ahead.

There's another print.

I follow it with my eyes, spotting another one just in front of it. The trail leads deep into the forest. I picture a giant human with a wolf's head prowling through the thick swamp, and I shiver.

'Did you make the prints?' I ask her, squinting, examining her.

'No. I swear on my life,' she says. 'Me and Grace found them together. At the same time.'

'Really? You're telling the truth?'

'Five hundred per cent.'

'That's not a thing,' I say. 'Percentages don't work like that.'

'Maybe I meant it metaphorically,' she replies, and sticks out her tongue.

I stare at her quizzically. Avery ignores me and squats to examine the prints again, edging as close as possible without stepping on them. The way her nose crinkles as she focuses her gaze tells me that she really thinks they're real.

'Fine,' I say. 'I believe you. You didn't make the prints.' I rack my brain to figure out what could have.

Was it a bear? The wrong shape. *A giant raccoon?*

They do have thumbs and five toes.

But a giant raccoon sounds just as scary as a loup-garou.

Sweat gathers on my forehead. The sun is high in the sky. It's already midday.

'We've got to go home,' I say, wiping it away with my sleeve. 'You know Mom will blame me if we're late.'

'Wait, don't you think the footprints lead somewhere?' asks Avery.

'We'll come back later,' I say. She nods.

'Here, we should take a picture. Just in case they disappear before we can come back. We can research it when we get home. See if there are any animals that have this kind of print.' I hand her my scratched-up phone and she crouches and takes a picture of them.

We push past the veil of moss and run back through the swamp, flying over rocks and ducking under low branches. I leap across the islands and dodge some turtles gathered on a log. We reach the kayaks and push them into the water, before climbing in.

'Want to race?' Avery challenges me with a smile.